Windmills and Wooden Shoes

Crystal Bowman

Illustrated by Joel E. Tanis

To Carolyn –
Enjoy!

Crystal Bowman

to Carolyn –
tip toe through the tulips...

CYGNET PUBLISHING COMPANY
GRAND RAPIDS, MICHIGAN

Requests for permission to make copies
of any part of the work should be mailed to
Cygnet Publishing Company
P.O. Box 6187
Grand Rapids, MI 49516

ISBN: 0-9636050-2-X

Edited by Julie Ackerman Link, Blue Water Ink
Cover Design by Tammy Johnson, Flat River Graphics
Special thanks to Karen DeYoung and Ann Mitchell

Produced in cooperation with
the Holland Tulip Time Festival, Inc.
Board of Directors of Holland, Michigan.
Tulip Time is a registered trademark of
the Holland Tulip Time Festival, Inc.

Printed in the United States of America
99 00 01 02 03 04 05 / DP / 10 9 8 7 6 5 4 3 2 1

To Ruthie, for her inspiration and encouragement; to Karen, for reading my books to her students; to Del, for letting me carry his sailboat in the parade; and to my parents, for teaching me to appreciate my Dutch heritage.

— C.B.

To my community: from Washington School to Third Reformed, to HHS, YL, Hope, 15th and Pine, and everything in between. Special thanks to the Kamphuis and Segrist families.

— J.E.T.

SOMETHING magical happens every year in the month of May in the city of Holland, Michigan. Slowly and quietly, millions of tulips push their way out of the soil, decorating the landscape with brilliant shades of red, purple, yellow, and orange. Then, when the tulips are in full bloom, boys and girls, moms and dads, and grandpas and grandmas from all over the world come to the city to celebrate the Tulip Time Festival.

There was a young boy named Colin whose grandmother lived in the city of Holland. Every year she sent him a Tulip Time postcard and told him all about the festival.

ONE year, Colin's mom and dad decided to visit Grandma DeHaan during Tulip Time. Colin could hardly wait to see the big windmill from the Netherlands, to hear the music from the marching bands, and to watch the klompen dancers in their colorful Dutch costumes and shoes made from wood. He was glad he'd been saving his allowance for a whole year, so that he had enough money to buy something really special.

"Welcome to Holland!" said Grandma DeHaan as she greeted everyone with a big warm hug.

"Where's the Tulip Festival?" asked Colin.

"It's everywhere!" said Grandma. "Today we're going to Kinderplaats. It's just for kids, but Mom and Dad may come along too."

THE park was a flurry of activities. People hustled and bustled from here to there, listening to music and watching the dancers. There were Korean dancers in exotic gowns, Hispanic dancers twirling colorful skirts, and klompen dancers wearing Dutch costumes with long aprons and the funniest looking shoes Colin had ever seen.

"Why do they wear wooden shoes?" asked Colin.

"A long time ago in the Netherlands, leather was expensive and hard to find," explained Grandma DeHaan. "So the people decided to carve shoes from wood to keep their feet warm and dry."

"Don't they hurt their feet?" Colin wanted to know.

"Not when they wear lots and lots of socks," answered Grandma.

Colin wiggled his toes inside his tennis shoes, wondering what it would feel like to wear a pair of wooden shoes.

THE next stop for Colin was the face-painting tent.

"I'll have a purple tulip, please," Colin said to the woman with the paint brush.

Colin wrinkled his face as the silky hairs of the artist's brush tickled his cheek.

"Oops!" said the artist as she wiped a green smudge of paint from Colin's cheek. "You almost got an extra leaf on your tulip!"

As they walked through the park, they came to a petting zoo with lots of animals.

"Grunt, scrunt, snort!" went a fat pink pig when Colin patted his back. Then Colin buried his fingers in the thick wool of a friendly sheep while a hungry goat nibbled Colin's shoelaces.

By the end of the day, Colin had collected a fist-full of bouncy balloons and a bag full of prizes. And he didn't even have to spend any of his allowance.

Colin went to bed that night feeling tired and happy all at the same time. He could hardly wait till morning.

SUNDAY was just the right day to go to a Dutch church service, which is exactly what Colin did after eating a breakfast of sunny-side-up eggs and thin, juicy slices of ham.

"Velkom," said a friendly greeter as they entered a church with big white pillars.

Soon after the service started, Colin began wiggling in the pew. It was very hard to sit still since he couldn't understand one single word. Grandma gave him a pink peppermint candy, a small pad of paper, and a little yellow pencil. As he sucked his peppermint, Colin held the pencil between his fingers and drew the outline of a wooden shoe. On the bottom of the page he wrote the letters: WOODEN SHO —. Just as he was about to write the letter E, he heard a loud AMEN! and all the people got up to leave.

After church, Dad wanted to go to the museum. "We can walk from here," said Grandma DeHaan. "It's not very far."

On the way, they walked through a park filled with talkative visitors taking pictures of the pretty tulips and resting on benches in the gazebo. Colin stopped by a pond to watch three large goldfish swim to the top. As they opened and closed their mouths they created little bubbles that popped on the surface of the water.

COLIN held Grandma's hand as they crossed the street and walked up the steps into the museum. There were so many fascinating things. Colin didn't know where to look first. He watched horses going up and down and around and around on a miniature carousel. He looked at the soft furry animal skins that hung from the wall. He stood next to a pair of huge elephant tusks. Then he saw a shiny black car with big round skinny wheels.

"I wish I had enough money to buy one of those!" Colin exclaimed.

"So do I!" said Dad. "That's a Model T Ford—one of the first cars ever made."

Grandma and Mom went to the gift shop to buy postcards. Colin picked up a toy car like the Model T Ford. A-a-o-o-g-a, went the horn when he pressed it. But Colin decided not to spend his allowance. Not just yet.

Colin went to bed that night feeling tired and happy all at the same time. He could hardly wait till morning.

MONDAY was just the right day to visit the windmill, which is exactly what Colin did after eating a breakfast of crispy corn flakes and creamy vanilla yogurt.

Up, over the long white draw bridge, past brightly colored flags flapping and flying in the wind, and down at the end of the path stood the old DeZwaan Windmill. The closer Colin got to the windmill, the bigger it looked. The tall brick tower had four long sails that turned with the wind.

INSIDE the windmill, Colin saw burlap sacks filled with grain lying in a heap on the floor. Long, thick ropes hung from the top floor, ready to hoist the sacks of grain all the way to the top. Up, up, up, Colin climbed the stairs to the grinding floor and saw where the grain would be ground into flour.

"When the wind turns the sails, the gears turn the grinding stone which grinds the wheat seeds into flour," explained Grandma. "The flour slides down a chute and is stored in bins until it's put into bags."

When they went to the gift shop, Grandma bought two bags of whole wheat graham flour that had been ground at the windmill. Mom bought a silver spoon with a tiny red windmill on the tip of the handle. Its sails turned just like the real one. Colin picked up a kaleidoscope with a picture of a windmill painted on the side. He peered through the tiny hole, watching the designs change as he turned it around. Then he put it back down. He decided not to spend his allowance. Not quite yet.

Colin went to bed that night feeling tired and happy all at the same time. He could hardly wait till morning.

TUESDAY was just the right day to visit a Dutch village, which is exactly what Colin did after eating a breakfast of flaky buttermilk biscuits, baked apples, and slices of cheese. As they entered the village, the loud cheerful music from the street organ welcomed the visitors. Colin saw a carousel just like the one at the museum—only this one was big enough for him to ride! He climbed onto a white painted horse with a bright red saddle. Then up and down, around and around he went, waving to Grandma and Mom and Dad at every turn.

"WHAT'S that?" asked Colin, pointing to a large contraption with swings hanging at the ends of long chains.

"That's the chair swing," said Mom. "Want to go for a ride?"

Colin hurried to get in line, then climbed into one of the chairs. Slowly the chairs started going around and around. Soon he was going higher and higher and the people below were getting smaller and smaller. Faster and faster went the chair swing, making Colin's head feel dizzy and whizzy, and making his stomach feel like getting rid of the biscuits, apples, and cheese he had eaten for breakfast. But just in time the ride came to an end and the swings slowly dropped down, bringing Colin back to the ground.

A group of klompen dancers entertained the crowd as Colin watched and listened to their wooden shoes. *Clip, clap, clop!* went the wooden shoes as the dancers hopped and stepped to the music from the street organ. *How can they dance in those heavy wooden shoes?* Colin wondered as he wiggled his toes inside his tennis shoes.

In the gift shop, Mom and Grandma each bought a white lace doily. Dad bought the biggest box of Dutch chocolate candy he could find. Colin looked at a blue and yellow street organ that played music when he turned the crank. But he decided to save his allowance for something else.

Colin went to bed that night feeling tired and happy all at the same time. He could hardly wait till morning.

WEDNESDAY was just the right day for going downtown to watch a parade, which is exactly what Colin did after eating a breakfast of fluffy blueberry pancakes drenched in warm maple syrup.

The sidewalks and curbs were covered with thick woolen blankets, sturdy camp stools, and lawn chairs of every size, shape, and color. Everyone in town wanted a good seat for the parade.

"Here's our spot," said Grandma DeHaan, pointing to the red-plaid blanket she had spread out on the curb earlier that morning.

Colin waited and waited and waited and waited. When he listened as hard as he could, he thought he could hear the drummers beating their drums.

"I think I hear the parade coming!" Colin shouted.

Then he waited and waited and waited some more. When he leaned over as far as he could, he thought he could see the parade coming.

"It's almost here!" Colin exclaimed.

Colin waited just a little bit longer, and then the parade was right in front of him.

"The mayor says the streets are dirty and must be scrubbed!" hollered the Town Crier as he rang a bell above his head.

Behind the Town Crier were grown-ups and kids dressed in Dutch costumes, throwing buckets of water on the streets and scrubbing them with long-handled brooms.

Grandma DeHaan started laughing. "I remember the time they tried using soap," she explained. "Bubbles and suds were everywhere. What a disaster!"

THE Grand Marshal of the Volksparade followed the street scrubbers. Riding in a white, horse-drawn carriage, he waved happily at the friendly crowd.

Then came the Holland High School marching band wearing red, white, and black uniforms and wooden shoes. They danced and marched to the tune of "Tiptoe through the Tulips" while the crowd cheered with delight. *How can they march in those hard wooden shoes?* Colin wondered as he wiggled his toes inside his tennis shoes.

A fancy float went by with girls in pretty dresses followed by rows of majorettes tossing and twirling silver batons. *Boom! Boom! Boom!* went the bass drum as another band marched by, and Colin felt the pounding in his chest.

After the parade, it was time to browse in some of the downtown shops. Mom and Grandma each bought a Tulip Time t-shirt, and Dad bought a Michigan pin shaped like a mitten. Colin pounded on a rubber drum and tooted a little yellow horn, but he decided not to buy either one.

Colin went to bed that night feeling tired and happy all at the same time. He could hardly wait till morning.

THURSDAY was just the right day to see another parade, which is exactly what Colin did after eating a breakfast of hot corn muffins and a small bite of fried liverwurst from Grandma DeHaan's plate.

The downtown curbs were covered with blankets and stools and chairs — just like the day before. Grandma had her red-plaid blanket on the curb — just like the day before. Colin sat on the blanket and waited and waited and waited — just like the day before. And finally, the parade began — just like the day before.

There were rows and rows and rows of boys and girls in the parade that day. They all wore Dutch costumes and carried tulips, flags, or something special they had made in school.

Some of the kids wore tennis shoes with their Dutch costumes, but many of them wore wooden shoes. *How can they walk in those stiff wooden shoes?* Colin wondered as he wiggled his toes inside his tennis shoes.

After the parade, Grandma bought four sticky, gooey caramel apples and handed one to Colin. He opened his mouth as wide as he could and took a bite. A blob of caramel stuck to the tip of his nose, and apple juice trickled down his chin.

Colin went to bed that night feeling tired and happy all at the same time. He could hardly wait till morning.

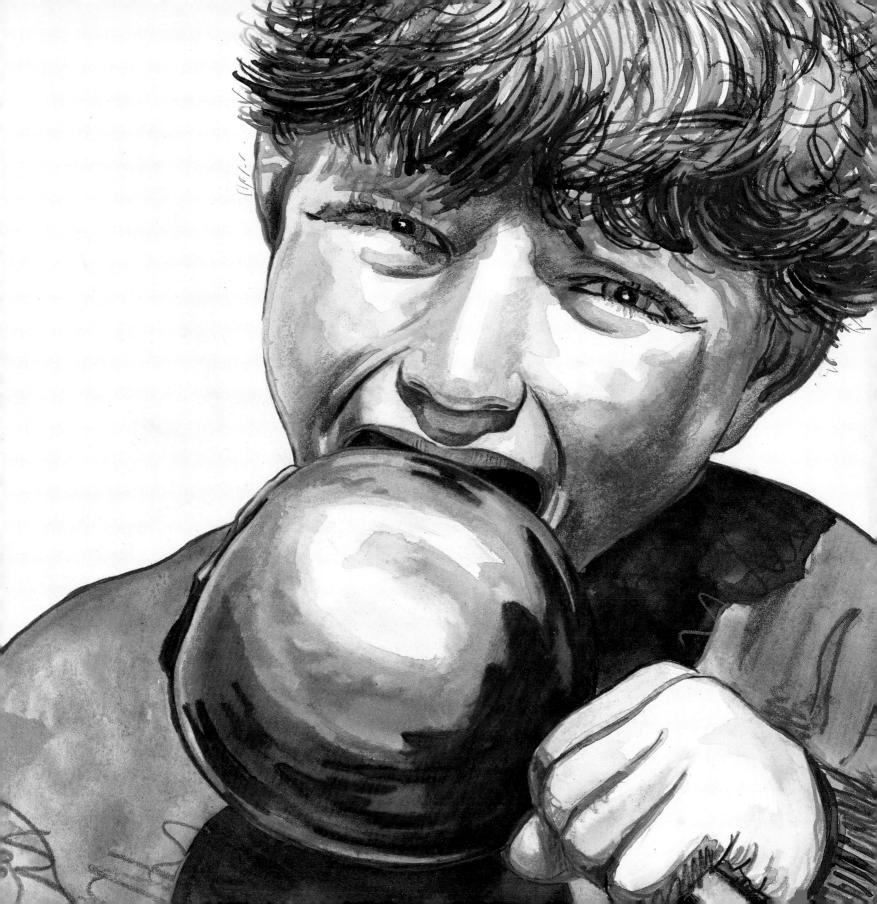

FRIDAY was just the right day to visit a tulip farm, which is exactly what Colin did after eating a breakfast of soft-boiled eggs and whole-wheat toast sprinkled with cinnamon and sugar.

At the tulip farm, Colin saw tulips of all shapes and colors. There were orange and yellow tulips with soft frilly edges, bright red tulips with sharp pointed petals, and deep purple tulips with smooth rounded petals. Colin bent down to take a closer look.

"Where do all these tulips come from?" Colin wanted to know.

"The tulip bulbs are planted in the fall," explained Grandma DeHaan. "They grow under the ground during the cold winter months and pop out of the ground in the spring."

"Now I know why they call it Tulip Time!" exclaimed Colin.

Next to the tulip farm Colin watched a woman in a Dutch costume paint pretty blue pictures on a white china vase. Grandma called it delftware.

Mom bought a bowl and a plate at the gift shop. Grandma bought a teapot. Dad and Colin just tried not to touch anything that would break.

Colin went to bed that night feeling tired and happy all at the same time. He could hardly wait till morning.

SATURDAY was the just the right day for a big surprise, which is exactly what Colin got after eating a breakfast of oatmeal and toasted raisin bread.

"Hop in the car," Grandma said to Colin. But she wouldn't tell him where they were going.

After a short ride, Grandma announced, "Here we are!" They got out of the car and walked into a neat, clean building. "This is where they make wooden shoes."

Colin watched with wide eyes as a man in a Dutch costume explained how wooden shoes are made.

"We start with a block of poplar wood," he said. "Then we chop it with a hatchet and shave it and shape it with a knife."

Chunks and curls of wood dropped to the floor as the man carved the block of wood with a long, skinny knife.

"AFTER we hollow out the inside," the man continued, "we let it dry."

Colin looked at the rows and rows of shoes on the shelves.

"Would you like to try a pair?" asked the man.

"Sure!" answered Colin.

Colin took off his tennis shoes and slipped his feet into the wooden shoes—first the right one and then the left. He wiggled his toes inside the big, heavy shoes.

"So this is what they feel like!" exclaimed Colin as he walked around the room in the stiff shoes. "Now I know why they wear so many socks." Colin slid his hand into his pocket and took out the allowance he had saved for a whole year. "I want to buy these wooden shoes," he said.

"A pair of wooden shoes it is!" said the man. He took Colin's money and gave him the wooden shoes.

BACK at Grandma's house, Colin put on every pair of socks he had in his suitcase. He wanted to wear his wooden shoes for the rest of the day.

Clip, clop! Every place Colin walked his shoes made noise. Out of the house. Clip, clop. Down the driveway. Clip, clop. Across the street. Clip, clop. And down the sidewalk to the spot on the curb where Grandma had spread her red-plaid blanket.

There was one more parade, and this was the biggest and best of all! More bands to listen to and more floats to admire. Giant balloons, antique cars, and roaring motorcycles filled the streets. A Spanish rider on a silver-white horse tipped his big-brimmed hat to the crowd. And the klompen dancers clipped and clopped their wooden shoes as they danced one more time for the boys and girls, moms and dads, and grandpas and grandmas.

Colin went to bed that night feeling happy and sad all at the same time. He was happy that he had a new pair of wooden shoes, but sad because tomorrow he had to go home.

THE next morning Grandma made pigs-in-the-blanket for breakfast. Colin imagined little pink pigs wrapped in a tiny red-plaid blanket, but that is not what he had for breakfast. Grandma's pigs-in-the-blanket turned out to be fat, juicy sausages wrapped in soft, flaky crust. Colin dipped his into a big blob of ketchup before putting it into his mouth.

After breakfast, Colin gave Grandma DeHaan a big warm hug before getting into the car. As Dad drove out of the driveway, Colin waved good-bye to the tulips in front of Grandma's house.

As they were leaving the city of Holland, Colin saw the big windmill in the distance. Its sails were turning around and around.

After a long ride home, Colin went to bed feeling tired and happy all at the same time. He could hardly wait till morning so he could tell *all* his friends at school about the big windmill from the Netherlands and show them how to dance in his shoes made from wood.

Crystal Langejans Bowman was born and raised in Holland, Michigan, where she enjoyed participating in the Tulip Time Festival. "I was a majorette and a klompen dancer," she says. "And one year I got to ride on a float."

Crystal graduated from Calvin College with a degree in elementary education and studied early childhood development at the University of Michigan. She is a poet, lyricist, and the author of several children's books, including Cracks in the *Sidewalk*, *If Peas Could Taste Like Candy*, *Ivan and the Dynamos*, and The Jonathan James Learn to Read Series. She enjoys sharing her stories in school assemblies and teaching kids how to write poems.

Crystal lives in Grand Rapids, Michigan, with her husband and their three children. She loves snow-skiing with her family, going to the beach at Lake Michigan, and eating frozen yogurt.

Joel E. Tanis was born and raised on Tulip Lane in Holland, Michigan. His favorite part of Tulip Time was watching the wooden shoes crack and fly off the feet of the klompen dancers. Another fond memory is that instead of selling lemonade to the tourists, Joel sold drawings of tulips for five cents. In the seventh grade Joel was part of the rollerskate team for the marching band.

Since those glorious days, Joel has earned a BA in art from Hope College and is now a full-time starving artist. His work has been shown throughout the United States as well as in Nairobi, Kenya. When he's not painting, Joel likes to travel, volunteer with Young Life, and sing in a folk-pop band.

Joel's illustrations can also be found in *The Dragon Pack Snack Attack and The New International Readers Version Bible for Kids*. He lives in Holland with his cat, Kitty.

Joel and Crystal dressed in their Dutch costumes sitting in front of the street organ at Windmill Island

For information on ordering contact:
Cygnet Publishing
P.O. Box 6187
Grand Rapids, MI 49516
Or visit our web site:
http://www.cygnetpublishing.com